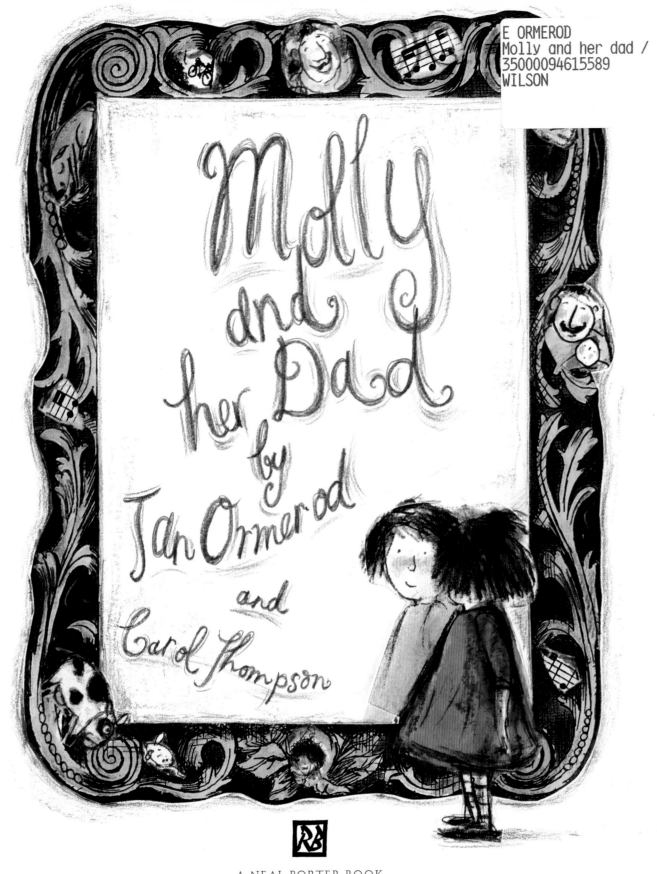

Molly and her Dad

by

Jan Ormerod

and

Carol Thompson

A NEAL PORTER BOOK

ROARING BROOK PRESS

NEW YORK

Text copyright © 2008 by Jan Ormerod
Illustrations copyright © 2008 by Carol Thompson
A Neal Porter Book
Published by Roaring Brook Press
Roaring Brook Press is a division of Holtzbrinck Publishing Holdings Limited Partnership
175 Fifth Avenue, New York, New York 10010

Distributed in Canada by H. B. Fenn and Company, Ltd.

Library of Congress Cataloging-in-Publication Data
Ormerod, Jan.
Molly and her dad / Jan Ormerod ; illustrated by Carol Thompson. — 1st ed.
p. cm.
Summary: Molly's father lives so far away that she makes up stories about him to tell at school,
but when he comes to visit she discovers that they have a lot in common.
ISBN-13: 978-1-59643-285-7
ISBN-10: 1-59643-285-3
[1. Fathers and daughters—Fiction. 2. Schools—Fiction.] I. Thompson, Carol, ill. II. Title.
PZ7.O634Mno 2008
[E]—dc22
2007047920

Roaring Brook Press books are available for special promotions and premiums.
For details, contact: Director of Special Markets, Holtzbrinck Publishers.

Printed in China
First Edition August 2008
2 4 6 8 10 9 7 5 3 1

For Angela
—J. O.

For Jenny
—C. T.

_M_olly loves to tell stories,
especially stories about her dad,
who lives a whole plane ride away.

Molly's mother says
she looks just like her dad,
but when Molly looks
at photos of him
she thinks . . .

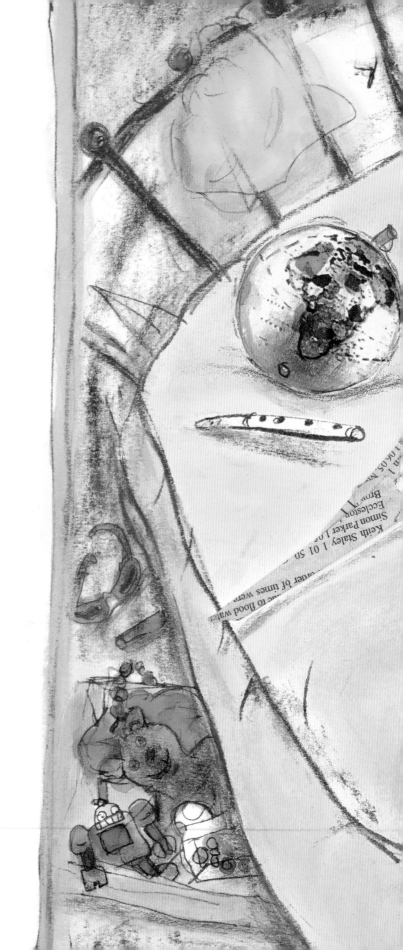

At school, other children's dads come to visit Molly's class.

Leo's papa grows things.

Maria's daddy brings them lots of paper to draw on.

Jasmine's pa can balance on a tightrope.

Woody's dad is a builder.

Molly tells her class, "My mom is going away for a week, and my daddy is coming to look after me—and it is not a story, it is really true!"

Then,
KNOCK, KNOCK!
DING, DONG!
It's Molly's dad and
he is big and noisy.
He smiles a big smile
and laughs a loud laugh.

Molly's dad cooks pizzas that taste funny.

He sings silly songs and
dances around the house.

Molly doesn't know
what name to call him—
Father, Papa, Daddy, Joe?
She doesn't call him anything.

The first morning, they both wake up late.
Then it was all rush and muddle.

w h e e e e e

Molly takes her dad into school to meet her class, and he tells them wonderful stories.

Just made it...

He tells them a scary story,

a sad story,

again!

more! more!

and a silly story about a cow and a dog.

And Molly is proud of her dad.

After school, they go shopping together and choose
smelly cheese and crusty bread and big bottles
of fizzy apple juice to share, and Dad buys
face paints just for Molly.
And now Molly knows just what to call him—
she calls him Dad.

They cook pizzas together, not too spicy,
and Dad calls her Molly.
They hang Christmas lights and
Molly puts on her party dress.

That night, they play loud music and dance
till the little house bounces, and the neighbors join in.

Later, Dad tells her stories about when she was a baby girl, until her eyes close and she drifts into sleep.

Now Mom is back home,

and it's time to say goodbye.

And now, when Molly says
"my dad" at school, they know
just what he is like—and so does
Molly. He is just like her.